Orse

the Moon and a
Piece of Smelly Cheese

Richard Allen

First published in Great Britain by Lollipop Publishing 2016

Lollipop Publishing Ltd,
141 Demesne Road,
Wallington,
Surrey SM6 8EW

orse.com

the polar bear

Orse, the Moon and a Piece of Smelly Cheese
ISBN 978-1-903774-02-1

Richard Allen and Jake Daw assert the moral right to be identified
as the author and illustrator of this work in accordance with the
copyright, design and patents act 1988.

Text & illustrations copyright © Lollipop Publishing Ltd 2016
Editor: Judith Paskin
Layout and text design: Lizzy Laczynska

Typeset in Bembo MT Schoolbook 14/24pt

Printed by Latimer Trend Plymouth

Orse

the Moon and a
Piece of Smelly Cheese

Richard Allen

Illustrated by
Jake Daw

LOLLIPOP PUBLISHING

MEET ORSE AND HIS FRIENDS

Orse, the polar bear

Kind-hearted and generous,
always likes to help the
folks of Snowville
where he can.
Generally gets things
wrong but usually all turns out fine in the end.

Eddie, the albatross

Local postman and not a
very good one at that!

Sir Stanley Walrus

Lord Mayor of Snowville
and owner of Windfrosty
Meadows Golf Club. Sir
Stanley has been known to
lose his temper with Orse.

Banjo and the huskies

All members of the
Snowville Rockets ice
hockey team. Banjo is
the captain.

Moosehead

Given his name because of
the shape of his antlers.

Sally, the Arctic tern

Wise and trustworthy,
often gives good
advice to Orse.

Frederick Rat

Lives under the floor
of Windfrosty Meadows
Golf Club and has
made a cosy den there.

Mauriceminor, the whale

Simply known as Maurice
to his friends. A good-
humoured fellow and
valuable foghorn for
warning of bad weather.

The seals—Bubbles, Millie and Kylan

Often up to no good
and causing trouble
for Orse.

Ohla

Orse's best friend from
school; comes to the rescue
when things go wrong.

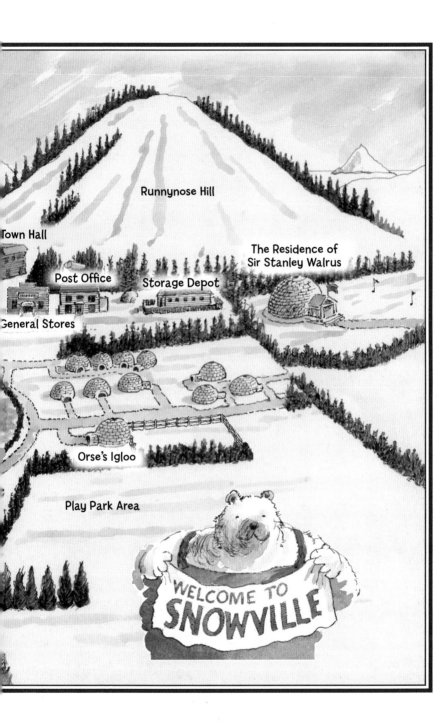

Runnynose Hill

Town Hall

Post Office

Storage Depot

The Residence of
Sir Stanley Walrus

General Stores

Orse's Igloo

Play Park Area

WELCOME TO
SNOWVILLE

For the children of the world, and me.

My eternal thanks to Jake Daw whose talent and skill
blessed my characters with the gift of life.
Richard Allen

Contents

Orse, the Moon and a Piece of Smelly Cheese

It was springtime in Snowville and the night air was crisp and clear with thousands of stars sparkling away quite cheerfully against a very dark sky.

Orse gazed up into space from the entrance of his igloo. He was an inquisitive polar bear, always asking questions and wondering where things came from.

His curious nature even landed him in trouble from time to time. The stars seemed to be winking back as he pondered what they were made from. Perhaps they were sugary sweets, or bits of special space-cake?

He shook his head and laughed. 'What a silly idea! Cake doesn't sparkle, does it? Unless it has those silver sprinkles on top . . .'

Orse began to feel hungry at the very thought of cake. He was rather fond of food.

A big yellow moon climbed slowly into view behind Runnynose Hill. His good friend Frederick Rat had often told him that the moon was made of cheese. This had to be true, because Frederick was an expert on absolutely everything. Or so he would have you believe.

Orse's tummy rumbled noisily, reminding him that it was almost time for supper. Just then he had a brilliant idea.

'Why don't I go and slice off some of that moon-cheese for myself? But how do I get up there? The moon does look rather high.'

At that moment, his phone rang. It was his best friend from school, Ohla. She was on her way to the trading post and asked if he needed any groceries.

There was a special offer on this week . . .
cheese.

'No, thank you Ohla,' replied Orse. 'I'm
going to get some free cheese from the moon.
I just need to work out how to reach it first.'

Ohla tried hard not to giggle as she said,
'Well, I think you're going to need a pretty
long ladder. Good luck and please be careful!'

Now more determined than ever, Orse started to put a plan together for his moon-cheese mission.

'Ah-ha!' he shouted, spotting his tennis racket propped against the wall.

'If I climb to the top of Runnynose Hill, I can use my racket to scoop up some chunky cheese for a feast.'

Soon he was ready. He climbed the highest hill in Snowville at a great pace, puffing and panting as he reached the very top.

The golden moon crept higher and higher in the sky; it seemed bigger and closer than ever. With a loud grunt, he jumped up and took a swipe with his racket. Mr Moon did not look at all happy, now that he had discovered what the bear was trying to do.

Whoosh! No luck that time!

Orse used all his energy and leaped as high as he could, stretching his racket upwards in a wide arc.

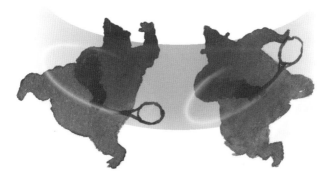

Whish! Still no cheese.

Mr Moon now
chuckled and
had a huge smile
on his face as he
looked down on the
disappointed polar bear.

Orse didn't much care for being laughed
at and so decided to leave
empty-handed.

Frederick Rat had
been waiting for
him to return with
a tasty supper and
had set a table for
two, ready for
the feast.

'Where is the cheese?' asked Frederick as Orse arrived at his igloo.

'I'm sorry Frederick,' replied Orse. 'I very nearly had some but I just could not reach high enough and besides, Mr Moon started to laugh at me so it was time to head for home.'

'Laugh at you, Orse? Well, we will teach him a lesson,' said Frederick. 'Tomorrow night you can go back with a stepladder and this time he won't be so quick to make fun of you when he loses some of his cheese.'

The next evening, Orse set off once again for Runnynose Hill but this time he took along the biggest stepladder he could find.

Puffing and panting even harder than the night before, he finally reached the top and positioned his stepladder ready to set his trap and collect some nice smelly cheese.

Whishhhhhhh went the first swipe!

Whoooooooooooooosh went the second!

But there was not to be a third!

Orse lost his balance and came crashing down on top of the steps, sliding down Runnynose Hill at great speed, riding the steps like a sledge . . .

. . . Whizzzzzzzzzzzz!

He sped into Snowville in a flash of white fur and icy splinters!

'H...E...L...P!'

he cried, realizing he was unable to stop.

Smash!
Crack!
Crunch!

Orse's ride came to an abrupt end as he crashed through the side of an igloo.

He landed with a thunderous thump, causing part of the wall to collapse.

'Oh-oh!' he groaned, 'now I'm in trouble.'

And he was right! For this was a special igloo. It was the home of the Lord Mayor, Sir Stanley Walrus who had been enjoying a tasty bowl of fish stew for his supper.

Sir Stanley roared, trying to sound dignified as fish bones, bits of vegetables and soup slid off his fur on to the floor.

'What is the meaning of this?'

'I'm so . . . sorry,' whimpered the terrified bear. 'I slipped on some ice and slid down so fast that I couldn't stop and . . . err, well here I am.'

Orse didn't dare explain about his cheese adventure and kept his eyes focused on the fishy mess on the floor.

The Lord Mayor was hopping mad. 'Look at the damage to my house and my lovely supper all over the floor! Now get out the same way you came in and make sure you are back here first thing tomorrow to tidy up this mess!'

Orse left Sir Stanley's broken home almost as fast as he had arrived. He  couldn't help giggling at the thought of the very important walrus with vegetables stuck to his face and whiskers.

On arriving home, tired and cold after his very busy night, he found a box outside his door. It was a present from Ohla—a large piece of cheese.

'What a lovely surprise! Ohla really is a good friend. But I think I've gone off the idea of cheese for supper,' he sighed. 'Perhaps I'll have it for breakfast instead.'

It had been a very long day, with rather too much adventure for one young polar bear. Orse was definitely ready for his bed. He smiled to himself as he laid his head on his pillow. It was the biggest, cheesiest grin you have ever seen.

Goodnight Orse!

The Swimming Race

Hooray! At last it was summertime in the Arctic. Winter had stumbled into spring and spring had blossomed into summer. The residents of Snowville were once again enjoying barbecues and garden parties now that the sun had returned from its winter break.

Orse was relaxing outside his igloo, reading a book about the Arctic games. Iceberg jumping, snowmobile racing and paw wrestling were just a few of the fun sports played at this special event every year.

He was also feeling very proud of himself and for a very good reason!

Earlier that afternoon, Orse had taken part in the school sports day and had won the sack race by some distance. The winner's medal hung around his neck and sat with pride on top of his warm white fur.

He was just drifting into a daydream about being an Arctic games champion, when three excited voices startled him.

The seal family—Bubbles, Millie and Kylan—had called round looking for a playmate.

'Howdy Orse!' called Bubbles. 'What's that you're reading?'

'A book about the Arctic games,' he replied.

The seals burst into laughter.

'Sports? You?!' cried Kylan, giggling behind his flipper.

Orse snorted. 'I could beat you in a running race any day of the week!'

'A running race, maybe . . . but how about a swimming race?' added Millie.

Without stopping to think, Orse agreed to the challenge, jumping out of his chair with enthusiasm.

The seals twitched their whiskers in glee. They knew they could swim faster than any polar bear and were sure to win with ease.

The excited
barks of
laughter
reached Sally
the Arctic
tern who flew
down and
landed on
Orse's head.

'Hey, what's all the noise about? Did someone tell a joke?'

Sally listened with a worried look on her face as Bubbles explained their plans for a swimming race.

She bent over Orse's ear and whispered to him, 'Seals can swim very, very fast. There is no way you can win this race!'

Orse gulped.

'We will hold a race around the giant iceberg in Bubblegum Bay,' declared Kylan. 'The loser can buy a bag of fish for the winners . . . US! Ha, Ha!'

The seals shuffled away. Orse could hear them smacking their flippers together in high fives as they left his garden.

'Oh dear, Orse,' Sally sighed, putting her wing around her friend's shoulder. 'Why did you agree to this race? Polar bears are good swimmers but no match for the fast seals!'

'Well they were making fun of me, Sally, and I wanted to prove them wrong,' said Orse with determination.

The day of the race arrived. The whole of Snowville was there to watch, waving flags and banners and mostly supporting the seals as they were almost certainly going to win.

There was, however, one noisy supporter for Orse. Tiddy, the little puffin, shouted and made more noise than you would think possible from such a small bird.

The Lord Mayor, Sir Stanley Walrus, prepared to signal the start of the contest. 'Once around the iceberg and back here to the finish,' he told the swimmers.

The four contestants lined up at the water's edge and Sir Stanley blew his whistle to start the race. **Peeeep!**

The three seals were off before Orse had even hit the water!

Sally felt so sorry for Orse. Those seals were very cheeky,  although Orse should have known better than to let himself be talked into a race he couldn't possibly win. If only there was a way she could help him . . .

She turned to Eddie who had taken the morning off from his postman duties to watch the race.

'Eddie, do you still have the football that you found washed up in the bay?'

'Yes, it's here in my postbag,' he replied. 'I was going to have a kickabout after the race.'

Sally informed him that they had something more important to do first. They both took to the sky in the direction of the iceberg.

Having reached the halfway mark in record time, the lazy seals sprawled on the iceberg, giggling as they watched Orse splash his way towards them in the distance.

They did not notice Sally and Eddie swoop down overhead as a football bounced across the ice.

'Where did that come from?' shouted Kylan. Without waiting for an answer, he picked it up and began spinning the ball on his nose.

The three seals couldn't resist playing pass the ball and showing off their balancing skills. What fun! As Orse swam steadily closer, he could see the seals were too busy enjoying themselves to notice him.

He gulped a huge breath of air, dived below the water and swam right around the iceberg. Once he had passed the turning point, he surfaced and charged for home.

Kylan was heading a pass from his sister Millie straight between the imaginary goalposts when they caught sight of Orse approaching the finishing line.

'The race!' they cried. 'Quick, hurry!' The three seals sped through the water, their flippers a blur of sea spray.

Back on the shore, the crowd had seen what had happened and were now fully behind the underdog, Orse. 'Come on Orse! You can do it. Come on Orse!'

Pushing through
every wave as hard as
he could, the polar bear
glanced back to discover
that the seals were closing in fast.

With a mighty roar, Orse pushed himself
to the limit and swam even faster. He just
beat the seals to the finish line by the flick of
a fish's tail!

Tiddy went bananas

and the crowd gave

a loud cheer,
'Hip hip
hooray for Orse!'

Lying on the ground panting, it took Orse a few minutes to catch his breath. He stood up and approached Sally and Eddie.

'Congratulations!' they cheered.

Orse was quick to reply.

'King of the sack race and now the swimming champion,' he proudly announced.

'Err . . . hang on just a minute,' replied Eddie. 'If it hadn't been for us . . . '

Sally quickly held her wing over Eddie's beak!

'That's right Orse,' she said, winking at Eddie. 'You really know how to win!'

Three cheers for Orse!

(*And four cheers for Sally!*)

Happy
Birthday Orse!

Orse was feeling restless. It was the night before his birthday and he just could not get to sleep.

He lay in his bed thinking about a tasty birthday cake with candles, birthday cards and perhaps even a present or two.

Orse had made no secret of it that he would like a guitar for his birthday . . . along with some cake of course!

It was no good, he was never going to get a good night's rest feeling so excited.

Although polar bears are very big and strong, Orse was as gentle as a hamster and could often be seen helping his neighbours prepare their igloos for the long cold months to come.

The winters in Snowville were always very windy with gusts of snow and ice whisking through the air and damaging the village's icy domes.

Repairing igloos could be hard work but
Orse quite liked to do
this as he would
sometimes get
a reward for
his efforts—
a few smelly
fish. Lovely!

Most of all, he liked to repair toys that had been broken by their owners accidently.

He had also designed and made a few toys of his own. He was very proud of the two-piece jigsaw puzzles that he had made.

At last, Orse's alarm
clock rang, announcing
that it was morning and
time for the post to arrive.

He gazed through the
icy window of his igloo as the sun crept higher,
painting the sky with pink and orange streaks
of light.

In just a few weeks the sun would take its
winter rest and not appear again until early
spring.

Suddenly, Eddie the
postman could be seen
soaring through the air.
Orse was quick to catch
his attention.

'Eddie! Eddie!' shouted Orse from
his window.

Eddie glided down and landed on the
window sill in a flurry of feathers.

'Hello Orse,' said Eddie. 'What's all the fuss about?'

'No fuss here at all,' replied Orse. 'I've been looking forward to receiving my cards today.'

'What sort of cards were you expecting?' asked Eddie. 'Playing cards or postcards?'

'No, no no, birthday cards Eddie! Today is my birthday!'

'Oh, well then, err, happy birthday Orse . . . now let's see what I have for you in my postbag.'

Eddie searched his scruffy-looking postbag, muttering to himself, but there was nothing addressed to Orse.

'Err, sorry Orse, nothing in here for you today, err . . . sorry. Oh! Goodness me, look at the time—must dash—no time to chat . . . bye!'

Eddie rocketed skywards, disappearing in another flurry of feathers, leaving Orse all alone with his disappointment.

'Has no one remembered my birthday?' he asked himself.

Sitting back down on his bed, Orse looked at his calendar and a big fat tear landed on today's date with a splash. Orse curled up on his bed and drifted back off to sleep.

Now it happened that Snowville had its very own ice hockey team called the Snowville Rockets, made up of dogs known as huskies.

The team were busy training for an upcoming match against a neighbouring club, the Salmonville Slurpers.

Banjo, who was the team captain, noticed that lying in the back of the goal net was a bundle of letters.

He read aloud
the address on the
top envelope—

'Orse
The Polar Bear,
Snowville'

Stinky the goalkeeper slid over to where Banjo was standing.

'I know what they are!' he shouted. 'Birthday cards! It's Orse's birthday today!'

Now it was clear what had happened; Eddie had lost them in flight and now poor Orse thought that nobody cared for him.

'Right,' said Banjo, 'this is something that we must fix straight away. Come on boys, let's go!'

The Snowville Rockets sprinted off towards the centre of town at top speed and were there in no time at all. On arrival, the huskies quickly gathered all of Orse's friends and neighbours together, including a very embarrassed Eddie.

By one o'clock they were all waiting quietly outside Orse's igloo. Frederick Rat had pushed his way to the front to get a good view.

Banjo thumped on the door. Orse peeked out, rubbing his eyes.

'SURPRISE!'

everybody shouted and Orse looked on with delight as the crowd burst into song, singing *Happy Birthday*.

The disappointment that he had felt earlier disappeared in an instant. His friends had remembered his birthday after all and some of them had brought along a few presents.

Yippee!

Ohla had tried very hard to buy Orse a guitar for this special occasion but with no luck.

Mr and Mrs Wolf, who owned the local trading post, had promised Ohla that they would have the real thing in stock before the talent contest in a few weeks' time. She decided to bake a birthday cake in the shape of one instead.

Eddie, who was feeling rather guilty, had bought a special present. It was a beautiful writing set with postcards from around the world.

Orse could now have fun keeping in touch with all his friends and family, although he wondered if it would be safer to deliver the cards himself.

He took a huge bite of birthday cake.
Delicious!

Happy birthday Orse!

The Talent Contest

Snowville was holding its annual talent contest and everybody was looking forward to the competition. There would be singers, jugglers, dancers and a special treat this year—a magician! It was all very exciting.

With just one week to go before the contest, Orse presented his entry form to Sir Stanley Walrus in person. Leaving this important task to Eddie, the slightly clumsy postman, was a good deal too risky.

'Good morning Sir Stanley,' said Orse.

'Ah, your entry form for the talent contest next week, I see,' replied Sir Stanley. 'Well, I'm afraid you're far too late to enter now.'

He pointed to  the calendar. 'The closing date for entries was yesterday.'

'But I've been practising my music and I only have to write the words now before the song is finished,' pleaded Orse.

'It's finished now,' said Sir Stanley, hiding a sneaky smirk behind his whiskers. 'Rules are rules and there are no exceptions.'

Poor Orse. As he left the town hall, he scrunched up his form and dropped it into a rubbish bin. What a disappointment. He had written a lovely tune for the contest and now he felt his hard work had all been for nothing.

Walking back to his igloo, he bumped into Frederick Rat who was very sorry to hear that Orse had got his dates mixed up.

Hoping to cheer him up a little, Frederick had an idea and said enthusiastically, 'Why don't you set up a stall and sell something instead, just like they do in shops? Perhaps some paintings or cakes . . . or maybe some toasted cheese sandwiches . . . yum . . . yum . . .'

'Ice cream!' Orse blurted out. 'Everybody likes ice cream and I know exactly how to make it. I will sell some ice cream!'

Well that was that! Feeling much happier now that he could still be part of the event, Orse continued his walk home, whistling his new tune.

On arriving at his igloo, Orse began to make a list of the different flavoured ice cream that he would offer for sale on his stall.

Everything went to plan and the night before the contest Orse packed the lollies and ice cream on his motorized sledge, ready for an early start the next day. He had even made a special treat for his friend Frederick Rat—some gravy-flavoured string—to thank him for his idea of setting up a stall.

The next morning, Orse's alarm clock, Tickerdy Tock, was not very happy at being called to work so early and looked positively grumpy.

Up in a flash, Orse washed his face, brushed his teeth and climbed aboard his sledge in no time at all. There was just one problem; the engine would not start and it looked like he would miss the contest altogether.

Orse put his head on his paws. Once again, it seemed that all his efforts were to come to nothing. Would things ever go right for him?

'Bad luck . . . all I ever seem to get is bad luck,' he moaned out loud.

'Luck has nothing to do with it Orse,' came a voice from behind.

It was Doctor Honk, out early to set up the first-aid tent at the contest site, just in case there were any mishaps on the slippery ice.

'How many times has that noisy, smelly engine failed to start?' he added.

'Well, err . . .' replied
Orse, 'now let me see . . .'
He rubbed his head,
trying to add up all the
times he had been let down
by his home-made contraption.

'Exactly!' a voice piped up from underneath
the sledge. It was Frederick Rat who had
decided to sleep there the night before so he
wouldn't miss the early start.

'It's not bad luck, it's a useless engine. Isn't
that right Doctor Honk?' said Frederick.

'Yes, indeed,' nodded the doctor. 'What you need is a reindeer to pull your sledge, just like the ones Father Christmas uses. Much more reliable!'

'I don't think Father Christmas would be very happy if I was to use one of his reindeer to pull my sledge,' said Orse, looking a bit shocked.

'And neither do I,' said Frederick. 'But I do know what we can use . . . **A MOOSE!**'

he shouted. 'There are plenty of those around and I will help you catch one Orse.'

'Yes, yes, yes . . .' stated Doctor Honk, 'but there's no time for that now. First we must all get to the contest site.'

The three of them set off towards the town square. It was going to be a long day!

Arriving a little late, Orse thanked Doctor Honk for his help and promptly started to erect his stall. Ohla was there to meet him and offered to help.

'Have you made a price list for your ice cream?' she asked.

'Wow, I knew there was something I had forgotten to pack,' said Orse.

'Don't worry,' Ohla replied. 'I have made one for you.'

The stall was finally ready for business but Orse was feeling rather nervous at running a shop for the first time.

The talent contest began and a large crowd gathered to watch the various acts. Frederick Rat performed his trick, climbing a rope while blindfolded. Banjo, the Snowville ice hockey captain, demonstrated how many pies he could eat within a minute—which turned out to be ten!

Everything seemed to be going well. Orse was doing a roaring trade and there was a long queue at his stall.

About halfway through the contest, Sir Stanley Walrus, together with some of the town's officials, approached the ice cream stall.

'Oh no, what have I done now?' Orse groaned.

Sir Stanley cleared his throat. 'It seems that one of the acts, a magician from Salmonville, has failed to turn up and the children are very disappointed. The committee has decided that if you wish to perform your song on stage, you may do so to fill the empty slot.'

Orse whooped with delight at this but then panicked when he remembered that he hadn't finished his song. He whispered to Ohla, 'But I haven't written the words to my tune yet . . .'

Orse was interrupted by Tiddy, the little puffin who was standing in the queue and had overheard everything.

'Come on Orse! You can make up the words as you go along. Don't you know that we are kids and we want to play, our work is done, time for fun, so what do you say?'

Ohla added, 'It will be fine Orse. I will stay here and sell your ice cream. You go and perform your song. Good luck!' She blew Orse a kiss which made him blush.

Sir Stanley led the way to the stage. Orse climbed the steps and was handed a guitar and hat on the way. He approached the microphone and started to play his song. He could see Tiddy, the little puffin, had made her way to the front to get the best view.

Orse looked at the audience and began his song.

'Well howdy friends, say how you doing there?
Some have short, others have long hair.
It doesn't matter to me either way
I'm gonna like you just the same.'

'The sky is blue and the snow is clean.
All the children like to eat ice cream.
Will you take the time to sing along with me?
Shall we sing it for your mums and dads?'

Orse looked at
Tiddy who was
trying to dance
to the music, and
grinned.

'*Don't you know that we're kids and we want to play?*' sang Orse.

'*Work is done, time for fun, so what do you say?*'

Tiddy was overjoyed to hear her words sung by Orse, and did a backflip to celebrate. Orse beamed at the crowd. He had performed his song after all!

It had been a long but successful day. While Orse was performing, Ohla had sold all of his ice cream and lollies. All that remained now was for the Lord Mayor to announce the winner of the competition. As Sir Stanley took to the stage, everybody fell silent to hear who had been voted into first place.

'Ladies and gentlemen, boys and girls,'  he boomed. 'Thank you all for supporting this year's event. And now that all the votes have been counted, I can announce the result of Snowville's seventh annual talent contest.'

Cheers erupted from the audience and Ohla gripped Orse's paw tightly.

'As you know, Orse the polar bear was allowed to perform his song, *And We Want to Play*, purely because another act had failed to turn up. Not having entered the competition officially, my view was that he should not be considered in the voting.'

Orse looked at Ohla and tried to blink back the tears.

'Oh dear,' she sighed. 'Come on Orse, cheer up. It was a lovely song and there is always next year's competition.'

Sir Stanley frowned and continued, 'However, it seems that all the votes that were cast were in favour of this act and therefore I have no other choice than to announce Orse, the polar bear as the winner.'

The crowd let out a big

HOORAY,

and threw their hats in the air. Orse and Ohla jumped up and down, hugging each other and laughing.

They turned to hug Banjo and Frederick. But Banjo was bent over, looking quite ill after gobbling down all those pies and Frederick Rat was far too busy eating up all the tasty crumbs that Banjo had left behind to even notice the celebrations.

That evening, Orse shared his good fortune
by having a dinner party for all his friends.

There was plenty of fish to eat, of course, but sadly he couldn't offer any dessert—all the ice cream had been sold!

At last it was time for bed. Orse gazed out of his igloo window at the stars. He thought he could see something being pulled across the sky. Was that a sledge? And what was that he could hear? A deep, cheerful voice was singing *And we want to play* . . . Could it be . . ? *Wow*!

Well done Orse!

TURN OVER THE PAGE • FOR A FUN QUIZ •

How much do you know about the world of Orse?

Question 1

What is the name of Orse's best friend from school?

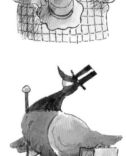

A: Frederick Rat

B: Sir Stanley Walrus

C: Ohla

Question 2

What is the title of Orse's new song?

A: Come Play With Me

B: Playing in the Park

C: And We Want to Play

Question 3

What kind of animal is Banjo?

A: A goat

B: A dog

C: A seal

Question 4

What is the name of Banjo's ice hockey team?

    A: The Snowville Rockets

    B: The Rockets of Snowville

    C: The Salmonville Slurpers

Question 5

What is the date of Orse's birthday?

    A: September 1st

    B: September 10th

    C: September 30th

Question 6

What kind of animal does Frederick suggest would be good at pulling sledges?

    A: A horse

    B: A moose

    C: A reindeer

Question 7

What is the name of the hill that Orse slid down before crashing into Sir Stanley's igloo?

A: Runnynose Hill
B: Big Nose Hill
C: Pick Your Nose Hill

Question 8

What is the name of the bay where the swimming race takes place?

A: Lollipop Bay
B: Candyfloss Bay
C: Bubblegum Bay

Answers

1: C   2: C   3: B   4: A   5: B   6: B   7: A   8: C

Orse's song '*And We Want to Play*' is available on ITunes and other Internet music sites.

Lollipop Publishing hope that you enjoyed the world of Orse. In the next book there are four more adventures from Snowville, including . . .

Orse to the Rescue:

Banjo and his ice hockey team are in big trouble and need saving fast. Can Orse help and rescue the huskies from great danger?

How to Catch a Moose:

Frederick Rat and Orse set out to catch a wild moose to pull Orse's sledge. Not an easy thing to do ... or is it?

Orse and the Magic of the Fairy Dust Trousers:

There's magic in the air at Snowville and Orse would like some for himself. But just how do you catch a fairy?

Ohla's Fancy Dress Party:

Orse is determined to have the best costume in town. But, as usual, things don't quite go as planned …